SECOND BANANA

Keith Graves

A NEAL PORTER BOOK
ROARING BROOK PRESS
NEW YORK

For Stanley, Barney, and Harpo

Copyright © 2015 by Keith Graves

A Neal Porter Book

Published by Roaring Brook Press

Roaring Brook Press is a division of Holtzbrinck Publishing Holdings Limited Partnership

175 Fifth Avenue, New York, New York 10010

The artwork for this book was created with pencil and digital color.

mackids.com

Library of Congress Cataloging-in-Publication Data

Graves, Keith, author, illustrator.

　Second banana / Keith Graves.

　　pages cm

　Summary: "A picture book about Oop, a gorilla, who is second banana to the Amazing Mr. Bubbles, a monkey, until one day, Mr. Bubbles finds himself in trouble and Oop has to save the day"—Provided by publisher.

　ISBN 978-1-59643-883-5 (hardback)

[1. Gorilla—Fiction. 2. Monkeys—Fiction. 3. Circus—Fiction. 4. Humorous stories.] I. Title.

　PZ7.G77524Sec 2015

　[E]—dc23

　　　　　　　　　　　　　　　　　　2014009899

Roaring Brook Press books may be purchased for business or promotional use. For information on bulk purchases please contact Macmillan Corporate and Premium Sales Department at (800) 221-7945 x5442 or by email at specialmarkets@macmillan.com.

First edition 2015

Printed in China by South China Printing Co. Ltd., Dongguan City, Guangdong Province

10 9 8 7 6 5 4 3 2 1

The Amazing Bubbles
was the star of the circus.

Oop was not.

The audience cheered
when Bubbles drove.

Oop helped
with the tires.

The audience clapped
when Bubbles dove.

Oop helped with the hose.

The audience oohed and
aahed when Bubbles played
"Twinkle Twinkle" on the piano.

Oop helped with the music.

And the audience went
absolutely APE
when Bubbles flew.

Oop helped with the fuse.

"I like helping," said Oop.
"But I want to be like the Amazing Bubbles.
Can I be the star of the circus, too?"

Bubbles chuckled. "You silly gorilla!
Think of us as bananas.
Obviously, I am the Top Banana.
The Big Banana. Numero Uno Banana.
You are Second Banana."

"Second Bananas are pool filler-uppers,
tire pumper-uppers, music holder-uppers,
and fuse lighter-uppers.
Second Bananas, obviously,
are not the stars of the circus."

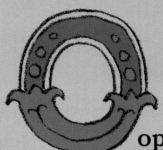op was discouraged.
She had a snack.
Snacks always made Oop feel better.

The next day, as the show was about to begin,
the Amazing Bubbles got a boo-boo.
"Heavens to Betsy! I have a boo-boo!" he cried.
"Obviously, I cannot perform with a boo-boo.
We will have to call off the show."

"Don't worry, Bubbles," said Oop.

Oop squeezed into the car and turned the key. The audience cheered when Oop sped into the spotlight.

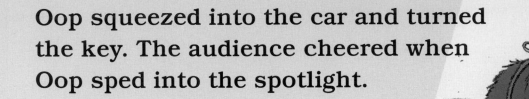

The car went faster and faster.

Oop could not slow down.

Oop tried diving.
She climbed carefully
up the tall ladder.
She inched her way
to the end of
the diving board.

said Oop.

Oop did not give up.
She sat down at the piano.
"I will play 'Twinkle Twinkle.'"
She had a few problems.
"Oops," said Oop.

Maybe Oop would have better luck flying.

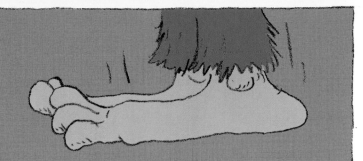

Far below, a pair of
skinny arms reached
up for her.

"Don't worry, Oop.
I will catch you!"
called Bubbles.

e did.

KER-SPLAT!

KLONK

"Oops," said Oop.
"Did I hurt your boo-boo, Bubbles?"
"Boo-boo, shmoo-boo," said Bubbles.
"Numero Uno Bananas always
catch Second Bananas."

"I'm really sorry," said Oop. "I crashed your car,
broke your board, pulverized your piano,
and cracked your cannon.
I was not a very helpful banana."

The crowd was cheering so loudly
Bubbles could barely hear what Oop was saying.

"WHO CARES?" said Bubbles.
"The audience loved it! You were amazing!"

"Does this mean I'm not Second Banana any
more?"

"Forget about bananas, you glorious gorilla!"
said Bubbles. "From now on we will be
the Amazing Bubbles and the Amazing Oop!"

"Wow," said Oop. "But now that I am amazing,
too, who will be the pool filler-upper, tire
pumper-upper, music holder-upper,
and fuse lighter-upper?"